Short Stuff

Short Stuff

A Collection of Flash Fiction and Drabbles

Jim Bates

Chapeltown Books

British Library Cataloguing in Publication Data

A Record of this Publication is available from the British Library

ISBN 978-1-910542-78-1

This edition published 2021 by Chapeltown Books
Manchester, England

Dedication

Three years ago my writing career consisted of me sitting in the basement working at my computer knocking out 12k word stories and posting them on my blog where I had an enthusiastic following of three loyal fans. One of them suggested that I join an online writers' group. Nervously I did, not knowing what to expect. Am I ever glad I followed my friend's advice. Through that first group I met some wonderful people, who led me to other groups where I met more wonderful people. To say my life changed for the better is putting it mildly. I began to learn more and more about the craft of writing. I pushed myself to be better. I also learned what flash fiction was and what drabbles were. With that in mind, I'd like to dedicate this collection of flash fiction and drabbles to my friends in those writers' groups. Your friendship and encouragement means more to me than I can ever say. Thank you from the bottom of my heart.

My favourite writers' groups:
    For Writers Only Clubhouse – Paula Readman
    The Cliffpack – PC Darkcliff
    The Inner Circle Writers Group – Grant Hudson

Contents

Introduction

When I first seriously began writing in 2011, I was drawn to poetry, primarily because of what I perceived back then to be its short length and simplicity. Little did I know how wrong I could be! But I persevered and challenged myself to write a poem a day for the next four years. Then I moved on to short stories, working diligently to learn my craft, something I'm still working on to this day.

This collection of drabbles and flash fiction are stories between 100 and 1000 words long. I think my commitment to writing poems back in the beginning of my career was in some way a precursor to me becoming involved in the creative challenge of the short form format. These stories are all near and dear to my heart. I hope you enjoy them.

The Mesabi Miner

The huge iron ore freighter was thirty miles out when Jerry Jorgenson saw it appear on the horizon, barely visible, a tiny speck. He pulled down his seed company cap to shade his eyes, and used his binoculars to watch as the ship slowly made its way towards where he was standing, close to the shipping canal between Lake Superior and the Port of Duluth. They say that death and taxes were what you could always count on. Well, to that you could add the Mesabi Miner, thought Jerry, as he watched the huge vessel's slow but steady progress. The freighter had been carrying iron ore back and forth across all five of the great lakes for seventy-three years, Jerry's entire life. It was as dependable as the day was long.

It took nearly two hours for the ship to make the journey, and as it approached the entrance to the canal it began slowing down, making ready to leave the lake. By now Jerry was surrounded by a boisterous crowd of men, women and children from all walks of life. Everyone was excited and the festive atmosphere blended in perfectly with the bright sun and warm sand and raucous seagulls. The huge vessel was so close he could almost reach out and touch its riveted steel immensity: one-thousand feet long, one-hundred feet wide and over fifty feet deep. It was fully laden with nearly eighty-thousand tons of iron ore, and it gave him a thrill beyond words to be standing so close to it.

The wheel house was seventy-five feet above the water. Unexpectedly, a figure appeared at the small window, leaned out and saluted good naturedly to those gathered below. It was the captain. The crowd called out and waved back excitedly. Not Jerry. He wasn't what you'd call a demonstrative person by any stretch of the imagination. Instead, he watched closely as the captain doffed his cap, expecting to see a grizzled and weathered seaman. But that's not what he got. He did a double take, and then had to raise his binoculars to make sure his eyes weren't deceiving him. They weren't. It wasn't a man who was doffing a cap and commanding his beloved freighter. It was a woman. And, even more remarkable, she wasn't even very old. He was stunned beyond belief. *What was going on? Was this a sick joke of some kind? What had happened to manly tradition and the stoically competent seafarers who were supposed to be safely guiding the huge iron ore freighters across the always treacherous Great Lakes? More to the point, what was this woman doing on what he always thought of as his ship?*

Jerry could not accept what he was seeing. It made him almost physically ill. Then as if to add insult to injury, the captain (that woman!) shook her head and set free long tresses of blond Scandinavian hair that shone in the sun like the finest imported satin. Her tanned face broke into a big smile as she gave the jovial crowd an impish wink and waved enthusiastically to them.

Jerry was aghast. *She's going to smash that ship, that's what she's going to do*, he thought to himself. *I'll bet my pension check from the steel workers' union that she's going to sink the Mesabi Miner to the bottom of the canal. Then they'll be sorry. Everybody knows that only men have the knowledge and skill necessary to make it through that narrow passageway and into the port beyond.* He folded his arms tightly across his chest in a huff, as if challenging her to fail. Then he watched and waited, expecting the worst.

If the young captain could sense Jerry's scepticism, she didn't let on. Undaunted, she turned seriously to the task at hand and, like thread through a needle's eye, she cool-handedly guided Jerry's beloved iron ore freighter through the narrow canal into the safe harbour beyond, completing the Mesabi Miner's journey by tooting its horn three times. The crowd erupted as one and began wildly cheering. Not Jerry. He turned away in disgust, the roar in his ears almost too much to bear.

He took two fast steps, and in his haste to get away almost knocked over a young girl about ten years old wearing a Minnesota Twins baseball hat. As he sidestepped her it occurred to him that his own granddaughter was about the same age. She was a delight to be around and was already an accomplished hockey player. It dawned on him that her mom, Jerry's daughter, was about the same age as the ship's captain. She not only was a wonderful mother, but also a highly respected veterinarian. Damn. It was a pain in the ass to do so, but he had to admit that the world he used to know was changing. Sometimes too fast for him, but it was.

He quickly apologized to the young girl who smiled and said cheerfully, "That's okay, mister."

He took a few steps and then stopped and thought to himself, *Hell, that lady captain actually did do a good job steering the freighter through the shipping canal, way better than I could have anyway.* His shoulders slumped ever so slightly as the realization hit him. *Yeah, she really was pretty good.*

He straightened up tall, having made what was for him a momentous decision. He turned and gave the departing vessel a snappy salute. Then he begrudgingly joined in with the crowd and began applauding.

Soap Bubbles

My daughter hands me the soapy wand and says, "Here, Mom, your turn." I take it from her and dip it in the solution before whipping it through the air. Allie watches mesmerized as the translucent bubbles form and begin to float away. Then she's all motion as she bolts from my side, running after them, giggling, trying to catch them before they pop and disappear.

Next to me Dad stands watching, arthritic and crippled by the years, yet eyes twinkling with life as he remembers, I can tell, when he and I both played this game. Gently, I touch his arm and hand him the wand. He takes it and reverently holds it for a moment, tapping it in his open hand. Then he confidently immerses it in the solution and, like an orchestra conductor with his baton, he moves it with subtle grace in a sweeping arc through the air. We watch as the bubbles come alive and go streaming, floating out on the soft, summer breeze, carrying with them joyful memories of long ago when I was a child and we shared happiness like this together.

Next to us, Allie is still, but for only a second. Then in a flash she takes off running with wild abandon, laughing and chasing our bubbles, while Dad leans his tired body against mine and we both watch, grinning.

Better Than a Sandcastle

The last time I saw the Big Jerk he took Mom and me to the ocean. They'd been dating for about a month, and to say he wasn't my biggest fan was putting it mildly.

"Here." He pushed me. I stumbled and almost dropped the cooler of beer he'd made me carry. "We'll set up right here."

Man, what a creep. I imagined spending the day with him and it made my stomach turn. Dad had died seven years earlier, just after I was born, and Mom was my whole world. Why she was putting up with this guy was beyond me. I guess it had something to do him being a father figure or something. *Thanks, but I think I'll pass.*

Except I couldn't. The guy had some kind of hold over her that I didn't understand, but on that day it all changed.

We'd gotten ourselves situated and sat looking at the waves crashing in on the beach while he drank beer. He regaled us with stories of how he was a hotshot executive in the entertainment industry. I didn't believe a single word and got the feeling Mom was starting to have second thoughts.

Then he started giving me a hard time, making fun of my freckles and glasses and skinny body. Finally, he stood up drained his beer and called me a pansy. "I bet ya' can't even build a sandcastle," he taunted, and gave me a look like, *what a pathetic little loser.*

He leaned in close and sneered. "I'll judge it when I get back and it better be good." Then he wove his way down to the waterline to go swimming. I pictured the tide pulling him away from shore so he'd be lost at sea forever, the most pleasant thought I'd had all day.

Mom looked at me. "I've had it with him. Let's get out of here."

They were the best words I'd heard in a long time. I guess Mom had reached her limit, and it made me happy, for both of us. "Just a second," I said. "I've got an idea."

I hurried up to the high tide mark and started collecting what I needed. It took a while, but Mom kept a lookout.

In the end, I built an elaborate sculpture, a three-foot-high pyramid made with different sizes of rocks all balanced one on top of the other. Mom told me it was magnificent and took a photo before we left. We never heard from the guy again.

The photo she took that day came out great: my structure with the different sized rocks looked stunning, especially set against blue sky with a line of surf in the background.

That was five years ago. Right now it's hanging on the wall over the sink in our kitchen. It reminds us of that day at the beach and the best decision Mom ever made.

Best of all, her new husband, my stepdad, loves it, too. So do I.

Good Science

Social distancing brought us together. It was the seventh week of lockdown and the governor had eased back on state-imposed restrictions about being in public places, so I took him up on it. My favourite coffee shop was open for walk-in traffic and take-out so I decided to treat myself to a fresh, steaming latte.

It felt good to stroll from my apartment for three blocks through a pleasant springtime morning and even better to open the door to Carl's Coffee and get smacked in the face with that roasted coffee bean aroma. Ah, it had been too long. Almost swooning, I moved into line.

"Hey, buddy!" A zealous manager suddenly appeared. "Six feet, remember?" He pointed to signs on the walls. In my excitement about being out in the world I'd forgotten the six-foot social distancing rule and berated myself for not remembering the drill. *Should I make a joke and play my septuagenarian age card with him? No, better not. Why push it?*

He pointed to brightly-coloured orange circles on the floor with "Six Feet" written on them just to make his point, a picture being worth a thousand words, as they say. I got it. Point made.

"Sorry," I said, feeling my cheeks burn. People were starting to stare. They were also wearing face coverings, something else I'd foolishly neglected to do. Mentally chastising myself, I stepped back quickly and bumped into a tiny woman who squeaked out an "Ouch" when I stepped on her foot. This was getting ridiculous. You'd think after being stuck inside for only seven weeks I'd at least remember how to act in public. But this was pandemic time and things were changing. Still…

I turned to her as I moved back to the required distance. "I'm so sorry. I don't know what's come over me."

Gray hair fluffed out over the collar of her jean jacket put her in the vicinity of my age. I could tell she was smiling because her amber eyes were twinkling behind her floral mask. "That's okay," she said, then quickly, and thankfully, changed the subject. "Do you live around here?" I was immediately impressed that she didn't get on my case for not wearing a face covering or berate me for clumsily invading her space, not to mention potentially injuring her foot.

"I do. I live just a few blocks over," I said, pointing arbitrarily behind me.

"That's nice," she said. "I'm in town staying with my daughter. I'm from New York City."

"Oh, my goodness, did you fly?" I was shocked. Getting on a plane at a time like this with Covid-19 running rampant seemed like an insane thing to do.

She smiled. "No. Well, yes." She laughed, understanding where I was coming from. "I flew in a few months ago, before the troubles…" (as she put it) "…began."

We chatted easily with each other, six feet apart, as the line moved forward. When we got to the counter, I turned to her. "What are you having?"

After a brief back-and-forth semi argument, she said, "Well, thank you. I'll have a latte."

Hmm. Same as me. "Two lattes, please." While the coffees were being made, I had an idea. "Say, would you like to join me?" I pointed outside. "It's a nice day. For Minnesota in the springtime, anyway. They've got their tables set up."

"Sure," she said, "that would be lovely."

I paid for our lattes and we took them outdoors. The morning sun was shining brightly, warming the day, and it felt good to be in the fresh air. We found an empty table, sat six feet apart, and made ourselves comfortable chatting and getting to know one another. It turned out we had a lot in common: we both liked to read, go for walks, cook and spend time with our grandchildren.

During a lull in our conversation I said, "Say, I don't mean to be too forward, but I'm having a wonderful time." She looked at me, raised her mask and took a sip of her latte, then replaced it. I couldn't wait for this pandemic to be over so she could leave it off and never have to wear it again. I'm sure she felt the same way. I looked at her sparkling eyes and smiled. She seemed to be waiting for me to continue, so I did. "I was wondering if you'd like to meet again tomorrow." Her non-committal look worried me. I was enjoying being with her and hoped she felt the same way. "Right here. For coffee," I added, just to be clear. *Was she interested?* She was witty and charming and it had been years since I'll felt so comfortable with a woman. "I'll even pop for a scone."

She eyes crinkled as she laughed. "Well, if that's the case, how could I refuse?"

Phew! Relief flooded over me. "That's great," I grinned. Suddenly, the pandemic was starting to feel not quite so brutal.

"There's only one thing, though," she said, as her daughter pulled up to the curb and beeped the horn.

"What's that?" I asked, standing along with her, wondering if I'd missed something and offended her somehow.

"Could you please wear a mask tomorrow when we get together? I'd appreciate it." She pointed. All around everyone was masked up. "It's good science, you know."

"Absolutely," I said, embarrassed. "I should have known better."

"Good," she said. "I'll see you tomorrow then, same time, same place."

I waved goodbye as she got in the car and drove off with her daughter.

One of these days, hopefully, soon, I'll be able to see that smile of hers. In fact, as I began walking back to my apartment, I found myself looking forward more and more to spending time with her. Her name was Sue. Maybe we'll be able to ride out the pandemic together and eventually not have to worry about masks and social distancing. I've got to believe that one of these days the restrictions will be lifted and she'll be able to take her mask off. I'd love to be there when she does. I'll bet her smile is beautiful.

Bloodsuckers

We were sitting on the city dock. I was crying. "I don't want you to leave."

He put an arm around my shoulder. "It's okay, little man," his term of endearment for me, his five-year-old kid brother. "I'll write every day." Ron was eighteen and my hero. Early next morning he was leaving to go to war.

Later we walked along the shore. I got covered with bloodsuckers and he sat me down and picked them off, one by one. I'll never forget his gentle touch, or how he dried my tears. Or that last day we were ever together.

Higgs Boson

Amy and I were graduate students at the university working with an elite group of scientists studying the smallest particle in the universe, the Higgs boson. Our project was to specifically look into how bosons were emitted at high speeds while traveling through the Large Hadron Collider at CERN, a process that involved using Feynman Diagrams. It was a dream come true for me and I was having the time of my life. Amy was working on the same project and we were both enthusiastic students. Maybe it was a shared love of all things subatomic, but something clicked between us.

"Would you like to go for coffee sometime?" I asked, after we'd been working together for about a month. I hadn't really ever dated much, being as committed to my scientific studies as I was, but, like I said, there was something about Amy that drew me to her.

She looked up from her computer, took off her glasses, rubbed her eyes and smiled. "Sure."

"Great. How's tomorrow sound? Say, after class?"

"Wonderful," she said and turned back to her work.

Well, that was easy.

For the six weeks I was the happiest guy in the world. Not only did I have my scientific research to work on (I mean what's not to love about analysing data involving z-boson trajectories and the Higgs field), but I was also seeing the beautiful Amy, who, with her short cropped auburn hair, blue eyes sparkling behind tortoise shell glasses and a figure that could only be described as otherworldly, had me spinning like a photon through an electromagnetic field. I was in seventh heaven.

But then… then Arnold Finkelstein entered the picture. Arnold with his wavy hair, perpetual three-day growth beard and hipster glasses. Arnold, the English major who wrote poetry and just happened to be friends with Amy's brother. Arnold, who apparently was everything I wasn't. I had no clue she was attracted to him until it was too late.

I'll never forget that day. The two of us were walking through campus from the lab to the cafeteria to get some coffee when Amy stopped, put her hand on my arm and turned to me.

"Terry, I've got something to tell you."

Oh, oh. I'd seen this before on television. Her tone of voice and her demeanour were not good, and here I was thinking that we were two peas in the same pod so to speak, two electrons in the same orbit. "What' up?" I managed to cough out.

"I'm seeing someone new," she said, with a dreamy look in her eyes I'd never seen before. "His name is Arnie," she fondly referred to him. Trust me when I tell you that I quit paying attention after she told me that he read his poetry to her and had taken her to the ocean to watch the sunset. How weird is that? She even told me that she was going to help him plant a garden. I pictured the two of them digging in the dirt, laughing and growing tomatoes or something. Man, what a complete waste of time.

So, she broke it off with me that afternoon. Of course, initially I was sad, but after giving it some thought for a day or so, all I could think was, *Good riddance*. You see, when it's all said and done, I like my sub-atomic world. It's safe. Predictable. Me working in a garden and growing vegetables? Or going for a walk along a beach and getting attacked by seagulls? I don't think so. Not when there's a world of bosons, and quarks and mesons out there to investigate. All I need is a laboratory and a computer and some data and I'm all set. Sit on a hill top and watch the sunset? Sorry, but I think I'll pass.

Sirocco Peak

To hell with her. His hands grip the jagged rock as he pulls himself to the top of Sirocco Peak. Gusts tear at his shirt as he stands on the edge of the flat stone mesa, six hundred feet above the desert floor. He loves it here. All alone. Wide open spaces. The infinite horizon. He spreads his arms and leans way out, his body buoyed by the relentless wind, wanting nothing more than to step into space and fly away. *That'll show her,* he thinks, just before he steps back, falls to the ground and breaks down in tears.

The Magic of Butterflies

In the instant before Annie passed away, her Fairy God Mother came to her and held her hand.

After she breathed her final breath, her Fairy God Mother held her to her bosom and said, "Welcome, my dear. Welcome home."

Annie looked at the kindly lady and wept tears of joy. She was finally pain free. She had never felt so good.

Her Fairy God Mother said, "Now, Annie dear, here comes the fun part. If you want to go back, you can. Do you want to?"

"Oh, I'd love to go back! Would it be possible to see Andy?" She clapped her hands with joy. "I'd like that so much."

"Yes you can. You can go and see your husband but there's a catch. You can't return as a human. You have to pick something else. Can you do that?"

Annie didn't have to think. "Yes. I know exactly what I want to go back as."

"Then it is done," her Fairy God Mother replied, waving her wand and dusting Annie with shimmering golden glitter. "You are free to return."

Oh, how the butterflies danced that morning on the summer breeze, drifting through the garden, keeping Andy company as he bent to his tasks. He smiled remembering how Annie loved them, even talked to them, whispering in their own ethereal language. Before she died, they would relax on their garden bench, butterflies drifting about, a poetic dance of daintiness, those colourful swallowtails, painted ladies, red admirals and monarchs fluttering among the flowers, alighting sometimes on Annie's outstretched hand.

His memories were interrupted by a caramel-coloured butterfly landing daintily on his shoulder. It stretched open its wings wide catching the warm rays of the early morning sun. Then it turned to him.

"Hello, darling," the lovely painted lady said. "Beautiful day, isn't it?"

Andy's heart quickened. For the past two years she had returned, and now this third time he finally realized it wasn't a dream. Annie really would re-appear every year.

"It is, my dear." He smiled and reached out to stroke her wings. "It's a beautiful day."

She tittered. "Oh, no you don't. No touching. It's not good for my wings." Then she laughed. "You know that, you silly man."

He turned serious for a moment. "I know, but sometimes I forget." Then he grinned. "Oh, Annie, it's so good to see you again. It's been so long."

"I know. A year. You understand, though, that I can't stay with you. I have to leave, right? I have to go through my change." She sighed. "But it's always good to see you and be with you if even for a short while. It makes my year."

"Mine too," he said, dripping some sweetened ice tea into the palm of his hand. "Here you go my love. This is for you."

She flew to his wrist and eagerly sipped up the amber liquid. "My goodness Andy, that tastes wonderful."

"It's sun tea with herbs from the garden. I made it thinking of you."

Annie flew up on a soft breeze. "You're so thoughtful." She brushed closed to his face. Butterfly kisses. "Come. Walk with me."

They strolled casually among the daylilies, geraniums, cosmos and sunflowers.

"Do you like how the garden is looking this year?"

She flew to his shoulder and alighted. "It looks wonderful, my dear. As always."

They shared the rest of the day and he was never so happy as he was now, when they were together. But, alas, all good things had to come to an end and towards sunset she flew close and said, "Okay, dear, I'm getting tired. I've got to go and get ready for next year, so I can come back and see you again."

"I'll be here I hope," he said, smiling, making a little joke.

Then he waved goodbye, watching as she floated away on the warm summer breeze. A tear formed. He'd miss her so.

He was taking a step to go inside when a stabbing pain shot through his upper body. He clutched at his chest, the world spinning away as he staggered forward, one step, two steps. Then all went black and he dropped to the ground. He died instantly. Heart attack, is what people said.

The next year the neighbours would remark on the two butterflies that could be seen in the area. A painted lady and a red admiral, flying close like they knew each other, never far from the other's side, like they were meant to be together.

And they are too, because forever and for all time they will be found on one day every year, the two of them floating from flower to flower, sipping sweet nectar and dancing their own ballet together on those soft summer breezes, winging their way to eternity.

Such is the magic of the butterflies.

Shape Shifter

Not many people know this, but we shape shifters don't get to call the shots. Most recently I was assigned to be one of those Covid-19 masks. That was interesting. I'm considered a very mellow guy in the shape shifting community, but even I got a little perturbed when the guy who was supposed to be wearing me stuck me in his pocket. Then he got sick. Man, was his wife ticked off. But things change. Now I'm a blaze orange maple tree standing in a park in the city. I'm really pretty. For some reason, people like me lots better.

Prairie Wind

Traveling from the east he came upon a tiny graveyard. It'd been nearly six hundred miles driving and, as he coasted to a stop outside the gate and turned off the engine, silence enveloped the car like a warm blanket. That and the billowing clouds of dust driven by the relentless prairie wind.

The old graveyard was situated on a low hill and located a mile outside the small town of Adair. He took a moment to collect himself, having driven straight through from Minnesota, following an uncontrollable desire to learn more about his great grandparents. And his roots. He lit a cigarette and smoked, trying to imagine what they'd gone through, traveling as they had, first from New York state all the way to Iowa and then across the great plains out here to the middle of nowhere. Nebraska. Their courage astounded him, Wyatt Plank, a guy who had yet to find himself, let alone set off on the type of perilous journey his great grandparents had undertaken in the 1850s.

He stubbed out his smoke, got out of the car and let himself in through the gate of the worn and rusted chain-link fence that surrounded the desolate, half-acre plot. Once inside he wandered aimlessly, studying the worn markers, marvelling at how old they are were and thinking, *doesn't anyone get buried here anymore?* Then he had a thought: *Maybe there's no one around to die and get buried.* For some reason the idea saddened him.

He continued searching until he found his great grandmother, a casualty of a wagon train heading to California, her stone battered by over a century of wind-driven sand and debris. He knelt on the compacted ground and put his hand on her battered marker feeling at once a mysterious connection with her. He read the faint inscription: "Katherine Marie Plank. Beloved wife and mother. Born 1824 and Died 1856". After Katherine's death his great grandfather had buried her on this spot and returned to Iowa with his three children, never to return. Years later after the town was settled, his great grandmother's lonely grave became the home of Adair's cemetery. How Wyatt's life might have been different if his great grandfather had buried his wife and then continued west.

Overwhelmed by the breadth of his family's pioneering spirit and that of his great grandmother in particular, Wyatt got to his feet and looked to the horizon. All around was the tamed land of corn and wheat fields, framed by an endless sky so blue it hurt his eyes. He pulled the visor of his baseball cap down low and, though he wasn't religious by any means, stood in respectful silence and said a quiet prayer for the courage of his ancestors.

When he was finished his thoughts were unsettled. He'd completed his quest, seen his great grandmother and paid homage to her courage and spirit, but now what? What should he do next? He didn't know. He was divorced. He didn't have any children. He had a job that he didn't particularly care for. In short he had nothing.

The wind whipped up a sudden gust and blew his cap off. He cracked a ghost of a smile, thinking that at least he had something to do. He chased it down, capturing it up against the western fence line where he put it on and pulled it tight. He was walking back to his great grandmother's grave to say one final goodbye when the wind shifted again ever so subtlety, causing him to lose his balance. He caught himself as he stumbled and wondered what was going on. A storm brewing maybe? But no, one look to the blue sky and the answer was clear: no storms, not even a cloud in sight.

The wind gusted again and blew a little harder, seeming to nudge him like a guiding hand, pushing him gently, as if it wanted to show him the way, the next steps to take. He looked to the west and watched dust devils dancing down a lonely country road. Beyond that, the far horizon seemed to call to him, drawing him in, like weather-beaten fingers tugging at his soul, just like they had for his ancestors.

It took him only a moment to decide. *Why not. I've got nothing to lose.*

He got into his car, started it up and left the windswept cemetery. He turned on the first road heading west. He'd made his decision and his path was chosen. It was time to complete the journey his ancestors had begun so many years ago.

He pushed the accelerator down, kicking up a plume of dust along the gravel road, the wind at his back speeding him along. He glanced in the rear-view mirror and caught his refection. He tipped his hat and grinned. He hadn't felt this happy in years.

Pancakes

Auntie Gertie spent more time that summer teaching me how to make pancakes than was probably necessary, but I was just a ten-year-old kid who'd rather have been playing baseball or video games than fooling around in the kitchen learning to cook. That didn't matter to Auntie. She had a way about her.

"Let's try to accomplish something useful this summer, shall we? I don't think increasing your score at Space Invaders really counts." She gave me a pointed look. It turned out she was right.

Earlier that year Dad had moved out, so Mom began working an extra shift at the local grocery store. After school let out in early June, Auntie put her foot down and said to Mom, "Kate, you bring those kids over here and let me take care of them." She lived five miles west of us, the next town over from Long Lake. "They can't be left by themselves."

Which was true. I was the oldest and certainly not the brightest bulb in the pack. I barely passed fifth grade. After me came seven-year-old Paul and five year old Shelly. It was definitely a good move on my mom's part to listen to Auntie.

The first thing she did was teach me how to make pancakes. I learned other stuff too, like how to cut the grass, weed the garden and be a nicer big brother to my siblings. But making pancakes was the first thing I learned and it was a good feeling, making something we could actually eat and enjoy. It was fun to make them, too. I liked to watch the bubbles form on the top. Like I said, Auntie had a way about her. She even taught me how to wash the dishes when I was done.

Looking back, it was the best summer of my life. I felt like I grew up a little. In fact, I'm pretty sure that morning wouldn't have happened quite like it did, if it hadn't been for Auntie and her influence on me.

It was just after sunrise the last week of August, a week before we had to go back to school. I came into the kitchen to find Mom at the table, a cigarette smouldering in the ashtray, a cup of coffee pushed to the side.

"Jeremy," she said, looking up and wiping a tear from her eye. "What are you doing up?"

It was six-thirty in the morning, the time I normally got up. I knew right then something was wrong and ignored her question. "Mom, are you okay?" I asked, pulling up a chair and sitting next to her. Mom never cried. Something big was going on. I wondered if it had something to do with Dad.

"Oh, don't worry about me. I'm fine," she said, standing up, suddenly a whirlwind of activity. "Let me get you some breakfast." She looked at the clock on the wall. "Go get your brother and sister. We've got time before I take you to your aunt's."

She went to the cupboard, opened it and stood staring. And staring. And staring some more.

I went to her side. "Mom?"

She turned, her eyes brimming with tears. They were the saddest eyes I'd ever seen, then or since. She put her hand on my shoulder. "Maybe you could fix breakfast today, Jeremy. I'm not feeling too well."

Nowadays I'd say she was almost catatonic, but back then I didn't know the word, let alone the meaning. She made her way to the table and sat down while I busied myself getting stuff ready.

When my brother and sister came in to the kitchen, I told them, trying to sound way more cheerful than I felt, "Big treat today, gang. I'm fixing us all pancakes." They barely cracked a smile. One look at Mom and even they knew something was up. But I fixed them pancakes instead of cold Cheerios and Paul and Shelly, to their credit, didn't make a stink. They ate them dutifully.

I even made some for Mom and she ate them, too. In fact, when she was finished she said, "Jeremy, those were the best pancakes I've ever eaten."

"Auntie taught me," I told her.

"Well, she did good."

In spite of the sadness of the morning, I think the smile that appeared on my face was the biggest one I'd ever had.

Mom called work and told them she wouldn't be in. Later that morning, Auntie came over and she and Mom sat and talked in the kitchen, drinking coffee and smoking their cigarettes. Mom told her that Dad had asked for a divorce. Not only had he left home, but he'd left home for good. That was the last summer we ever heard from him.

In later years, Mom always talked about how much she appreciated me making breakfast that day, saying, "You were such a great help, Jeremy. It really made things easier for me."

She always said they were the best pancakes she'd ever eaten even though it turned out I had forgotten to put the egg in. Auntie pointed that mistake out later that day when Mom had gone upstairs to rest. I'd made her some, too, when she'd come over.

"Jeremy, I can't believe you fed your mother and your brother and sister this junk. I thought I taught you better than that." Then she smiled and hugged me. "But, you live and learn. Right? There's always next time."

Right. There was always a next time, and I always got it right. But Mom never said a bad word about the pancakes I fixed for her that day even though my brother and sister sure did. I guess that's what it means to really love your kid. You'll forgive them just about anything.

Patchouli Oil

The stink of the diesel idling outside their apartment agitated the old man. His caregiver opened a vial of patchouli oil and wafted it under his nose. Instantly he calmed. A smile formed as he remembered the sixties, a long-haired, tie-dyed hippie in love with life and a flower child named Sunshine. Who became his wife. And caregiver. He watched as Sunshine breathed in the scented fragrance and put a scratched Jefferson Airplane album on the old turntable. Then she joined him on his lap and held him tight while *Don't You Want Somebody To Love* played. It was perfect.

Perfectly Harmless

Harmless. That's what the punk kid thought the old man was, sitting at a table by himself in the strip mall coffee shop. Perfectly harmless. He quickly slipped behind the counter and slid the edge of the razor sharp stiletto against the young clerk's neck, whispering, "Keep calm, honey, and I won't cut you." He smiled as he watched a tear form in the young girl's eye. *This robbery will be a piece of cake*, he was thinking. *No problem at all.*

Just then, all hell broke loose.

The old man noticed what was going on and it made him mad. He angrily got to his feet and started yelling and waving his arms, causing such a distracting scene that the cashier was able to press a button under the counter which notified security. In the few moments it took for them to arrive, she stomped down heavily on the punk's toe with the heavy heal of her boot and he screamed in pain. While all that was happening, the old man slowly but steadily made his way to the counter and began smacking the punk across the top of the head with his cane. It might have been comical if the young clerk hadn't inadvertently been cut by the robber's knife and was bleeding.

Two beefy guys from security showed up, quickly subdued the punk and held him until the police arrived. A nurse browsing in the nearby bookstore administered to the young clerk pronouncing that she'd be just fine, it was just a slight nick.

That left the old man, an octogenarian named Jack, who received a hearty thank you from the building manager, offering, "We could get you on the evening news if you'd like, Jack. Your fifteen minutes of fame? I could fix it up with the local station." He put his arm around the old man's skinny shoulder and sat him down. "What do you think? You want to be famous?"

Jack didn't have to think. He shook his head in the negative, and said, "Why make a big deal out of it, young man? Most of the people I know would have done the same thing."

The manager laughed to himself. *Yeah, right. A bunch of old people? I sincerely doubt it.* But to Jack he said, "Suit yourself. How about a free cup of coffee?"

"You're on for the coffee," Jack said rising to his feet, looking at his wrist watch. "But I'll have to take it to go if you don't mind. I have a bus to catch."

After he got his coffee Jack picked up his cane and made his way to the door, waving goodbye to the building manager, the clerk, the nurse and the two security guards. He was feeling good, better than he had in a long time. He couldn't wait to get back to the Orchard Lake Retirement Home where he lived. Tonight was their self-defence class and he didn't want to be late. Boy, did he have a story for them.

Fear of Snakes

We'd been dating for a about a month when Lorrie got a bull snake as a pet and brought it over to my apartment. "Here," she said, pushing the writhing reptile towards me. "Her name is Julie. Want to hold her?"

No. Not on your life.

But, I liked Lorrie a lot and wanted to make a good impression, so I attempted to work up some enthusiasm. "Sure!"

Bad idea. Julie was heavy and cold and thick and she curled around my arm, stuck out her tongue and maybe some more stuff I'll never know because I fainted. I came to on the floor with a warm blanket tucked around me and a soft pillow placed under my head. Lorrie and Julie were both gone.

I stood on shaky legs and phoned Lorrie right away. "Please come back. You can even bring Julie."

"You sure?"

"Positive," I gulped, suddenly weak in my knees, wondering what I was getting myself into.

"Great. We're on our way."

"Fabulous. See you soon!"

Oh, oh. I didn't even have time to think before my reptilian world went spinning around and around and around. I fainted once again and crashed to the floor.

A little while later, Lorrie's concerned voice brought me around, "Jerry,

Jerry. Are you okay?" I sat up, rubbing my eyes. "Yeah, I'm all right. I just… wait a minute!" I panicked, scanning the room frantically. "Where's Julie?"

Lorrie smiled and kissed me. "She's not here. I didn't want to take a chance on…"

"…on me fainting again?" I completed her thought, feeling not only sheepish at my inability to deal with reptiles in general and Julie in particular, but also relieved I wouldn't have to, at least not right then.

"Yeah, something like that," she grinned.

I felt bad. I didn't want this woman I really cared about to think I was being a jerk for not liking her pet snake; her beloved Julie. Also, there was that male ego thing. I wanted to prove to her I really wasn't all that afraid.

Next thing I knew, feeling a burst of confidence that came out of nowhere, I stated, "I'll tell you what. I'm willing to give it another try." I remember distinctly trying to keep the tremor out of my voice.

"That's so sweet," she hugged me. "Really?"

I took a deep breath and let it out. "Really."

"Well, that's great. I'll go get her."

"Wait a minute! What do you mean? Now?"

"Yeah. I left her in my car. I'll be right back."

Oh, my. What had I gotten myself into?

Five months later and I have to say that things are working out good. Lorrie and I get along great and are still dating. I'm getting used to Julie. We even play together sometimes. She's not so bad, although she's kind of heavy.

Lorrie feeds her once a week. I won't tell you what, but let's just say that I leave mealtimes to her.

But, when it comes to love? Well that's a different story. I care for Lorrie a lot and I'll do just about anything for her, even learn to like Julie. But please, don't let her start buying any more snakes, even one as likeable as her pet. I'm not sure I could handle it, because, believe me, as far as me and pet snakes are concerned, one is more than enough.

Freyja

As if Norse winters weren't bad enough, her dullard of a husband Oor didn't help. Gone all the time doing his macho thing, he gave gifts like a Brisingamen necklace and a wild boar, thinking they would please her. But no. She wasn't easily bought off. She had a good life all her own, ruling over the heavenly fields of Folkvangr and taking care of her lovely daughters, Hnoss and Gersemi. So, when he tried to placate her with a fancy chariot pulled by two cats, that was too much. A goddess like her? She at least deserved winged horses.

Why I Ate So Much

I never did figure out where the voices were coming from, but they were there, that was for sure, day and night, whispering, "Feed us. Feed us, now."

So I did. Boy, did I ever.

I was fifteen and Mom just thought I'd hit a growth spurt.

A typical day: a dozen pancakes for breakfast. A mid-morning snack of five candy bars. A hot lunch at school plus the bag lunch I'd brought. Then a stop at the fast food place on the way home for large fries, large shake and a couple of quarter pounders. Just enough to tide me over until I got home.

"What's for dinner, Mom?"

"Spaghetti. Your favourite."

"Fantastic," I told her, although at this stage of the game, anything I could put in my mouth was fabulous. One helping. A second helping. Dad sitting there with his mouth hanging open, watching.

I ask him, "Can I finish that?" and point.

"Sure," he says, as I clear his plate before the word is barely out of his mouth.

I wasn't growing or putting on weight, just eating. A lot.

After a few months Mom became concerned. "Let's take you to the doctor."

"Aw, Mom. No."

A steely look. "What'd you say?"

I re-think my position. "Sure, Mom. Good idea."

Doctor Solsvik was a kind man. We talked. He checked me over. Finally, he felt my abdomen. "Good lord," he gasped. "Let's get you to x-ray."

End result: I had a tapeworm. Two of them, actually. Big ones. How they got there no one knows. But the doctor operated and now I'm back to normal. "Eating like a horse," Mom says.

"I'm a growing boy," I joke, because I'm pretty sure those tapeworms are gone. At least that's what they tell me.

Tougher Than She Looked

She was a poet. She lived alone and often caught her muse by walking the streets of the city she called home.

Her friends cautioned her, "You need to watch out, Rose. The creeps are out there. Drug dealers, pimps and a hundred different kind of deviants. You're no match for any of them."

Rose understood. She was a tiny, waif of a girl and had experienced her fair share of run-ins, the most recent a three-hundred-pound guy with a shaved head and tattoos from here to there. She'd gotten away but he'd been able to nick her on the arm with his knife before she outran him. *Never again,* she thought to herself.

She knew it was dangerous on the streets, but she was also compelled to be there, to write her poetry. Tonight was a perfect night for it – the misting rain and coloured lights blazing from the dive bars and cheap pay-by-the-hour hotels. She loved the way the red neon danced through the falling rain drops, a city's soul illuminated in reflected light.

She hurried out to the street, composing a poem as she went. *The rain settles soft, muting hard edges. The streets are washed clean from the filth of the day.*

She walked faster, opening her heart to the city, alive with colour, inundating her with more images. *Red neon lights up the night, fleeting comfort for the lost and lonely.*

She was on fire with words flowing – a deluge. She was glad she brought her umbrella. She planned to be out for a long time.

Behind her she didn't see the big man step from a shadowy doorway. A bald man with tattoos. He chuckled to himself as he fell in behind her, fingering the stiletto in his pocket. "I've been waiting for you," he whispered, wanting her badly, even more so after she'd escaped that first time.

Oblivious, Rose splashed through puddles, more words forming. *Rain is the life blood of the streets, a harmonic heart beat thumping to the sound of thunder. Shadows are friends to those who love the night. They greet you...*

Suddenly she was grabbed from behind and a tattooed arm crushed down tight on her windpipe, gagging her, choking her. She tried to spin away but couldn't. Stale breath whispered in her ear, laughing. "You're all mine."

With a surge of energy Rose stabbed the metal tip of her umbrella into his foot, thankful she'd sharpened it to a needle point edge after that last run-in. He screamed and let go, but she didn't run. Instead, she turned to her attacker, stepped forward and stabbed her umbrella hard, jamming the tip with all her might into his soft belly. Then she stepped back and watched as he fell to the street, blood flowing, her next poem already forming. *She was a city girl at home in the streets, and she was tougher than she looked.*

Heroes

"I wish you could swim," Camden told Megan. "Like the dolphins."

They were downtown, sitting outside, having just finished lunch at a favourite cafe. She sent off a final text to her mother, set the phone down and looked at him like he was nuts. "Camden, what in the world are you talking about? I can swim, you know that."

"I know. It's just that I was thinking about after we're married and how much I was looking forward to getting away with you, especially from your parents. I know they don't care for me. They've said more than once that they thought nothing could keep us together."

"I know, honey. I'm sorry about that. And them."

"Me, too. But it is what it is, even though we've been a couple for over five years. I was thinking we could go to the Caribbean for a few days, maybe ride on one of those catamarans and go swimming with the dolphins. I've got some money saved up. It'd be fun."

"What brought this on all of a sudden?"

"Look, I know your parents wanted you to marry some rich guy, a lawyer or doctor or someone like that. Not…"

"Not a guy who teaches fifth grade in a hundred-year-old building in the dark and dirty inner city," she interrupted, finger quoting around dark and dirty.

Camden grinned. "Well, yeah, something like that. I just want me and you to do something special after we're married, that's all. Just the two of us."

Megan looked at him, her eyes dark and sensual, eyes he never tired of looking into. "Look, Cam, it's you I love, and it's you I want to spend my life with."

"You're saying that together we can beat them, forever and ever?"

"Yes, that's what I'm saying."

"What about your parents? They're paying for the wedding."

"I know…" she sighed. "We're just going to have to compromise, somehow, be nice and try to get along."

"Remember they also wanted to take us to Paris. Show us that new Monet exhibit."

"Which would be fun to see, I can't lie, but we're kind of stuck going there with them." She sighed and shook her head. "I have to say, though, traveling with my folks was not how I pictured us spending our honeymoon."

"I'm glad to hear you say that." Camden smiled at her, reaching out to caress her hand. "How about when we get back, you and I go to the Caribbean by ourselves?"

Megan snapped her fingers and looked at him, an idea suddenly forming. "How about if I tell my parents that it's time for them to let me live my life the way I want? How about if I tell them that we'll do our own wedding, on our own terms? How about that?"

Camden stood up, excited and pointed. "You know, the courthouse is right around the corner. We could get married there. Right now. What do you think? Let's do it."

Megan stood up, grinning. "Let's." Just then her phone beeped a text. She glanced at the screen. "It's from Mom." Camden watched, waiting, wondering what she'd do. It didn't take her long to decide. She put the phone in her purse without answering and turned to him. "Screw it. Let's go to the courthouse. I'll call her tomorrow. It's our life, not my parents'."

Camden knew exactly what that call tomorrow would entail. Megan liked her things. She liked to travel. She like Monet. More than anything he was certain the big wedding would take place and the trip to Paris would happen. But that was all right. Today it was just the two of them with a dream of the traveling to the Caribbean and swimming with the dolphins.

"I could be king and you could be queen," he said, smiling wide.

"That's right," Megan agreed. "No matter what happens, we could be heroes."

Camden, hugged her tightly, not caring about anything except being with her. He paid for their lunch and they started walking toward the courthouse, arms around each other, happy and in love. He looked at her and smiled. "That's for sure, Megan. We'll be heroes. Even if it's for just one day."

Transcendentalists

"The Transcendentalists lived in Massachusetts in the eighteen-fifties," Teacher said. "They believed that man could exist and be at one with nature. Examples would be Ralph Waldo Emerson and his friend Henry David Thoreau, a man who built a cabin on Walden Pond and lived there by himself for two years."

Larry Adams listened intently to his tenth grade English teacher and liked what he was hearing. *I could get into that*, he thought to himself. Never the best student, he enjoyed being outdoors. A lot. He liked walking in the fields and woods outside of town and drawing pictures of birds and wildflowers in his sketchbook. Mostly, though, he liked being by himself. He couldn't help thinking that maybe he was like those Transcendentalists. He smiled to himself. Maybe there was a little bit of that Thoreau guy in him.

Later in the day, when his math teacher started talking about geometry, Larry quickly lost interest. Fighting back a yawn, he tried his hardest to stay awake but just couldn't. He lay his head down on his desk and soon nodded off.

Teacher woke him by yelling in his ear, "Adams, you good for nothing! Wake up and get to work on your assignment."

"Yes, sir!" Larry said, as he snapped to attention, fighting back an urge to salute the arrogant so and so.

Teacher stared at him and shook his head in disgust, muttering, "You'll never amount to anything, Adams, you know that don't you? You're a loser with a capital L."

Well, to each their own, Larry thought, thinking back to the Transcendentalists. He liked the world they lived in. He opened his math book, but instead of lifeless numbers, he saw a rolling landscape of verdant forests and sun-drenched fields. There was even a hint of a secluded, faraway pond glistening in the distance. He didn't have to think as he decided to hike to it.

In a matter of moments, school became a distant memory as he found himself strolling through a land filled with colourful wildflowers and the delightful twittering of countless singing songbirds. He had a sudden urge to join them, so he did. Happily, loud and clear, he began to whistle a warbling little tune. It actually sounded quite pleasant, even if he did say so. He smiled to himself. Too bad if Teacher didn't like it.

Emil's Magic

He was standing off to the side of the city Greenway looking at the sky when he felt a tap on his shoulder. "Hey buddy. What are you doing?"

Emil turned. It was a policeman on bicycle patrol. "I'm just looking at the clouds, Officer," he said, politely. "That one over there reminds me of a bunny rabbit."

Unimpressed, the cop got off his bike and adjusted his crotch. "I see you down here a lot. Where do you live?"

"Nearby," he said and then tried to change the subject. "I just like to walk here," he indicated arbitrarily. The Greenway led from Lake of the Isles, near where they were standing, on the west end of Minneapolis, all the way east to St. Paul, a distance of fifteen miles. People walked and biked on it nearly every moment of the day.

"Let's see some identification."

Emil fumbled through his pockets and then put his tattered shopping bag down and looked through it and then shrugged off his backpack and looked through it. Then he did it all again before finally saying, "I'm sorry, Officer. I seem to have lost it."

The policeman smirked. "Yeah, I'll bet." He took his radio from his belt and made a call. "I'm bringing a guy in." He listened for a moment and said, "No, he's not drunk. I think he's delusional. Let's see how he does in lockup overnight and then we'll take it from there."

Emil couldn't help but overhear the conversation. "Officer, I promise I'm not delusional. I'm perfectly sane. I just like to walk and be outdoors."

"Too bad, buddy, you seem a little off to me. No more walking and being outside for you today."

He called for a patrol car and they took Emil to the station where he was booked for loitering and put in a holding cell with fifteen other inmates.

His jailer, a heavy set black man with a grey beard said, "Here you go, buddy. We'll come get you for dinner at 5:30. Have fun." He slammed the door shut.

Emil made it a point to avoid eye contact with the other inmates and shuffled to the corner of the cell. He faced the wall and closed his eyes and concentrated, letting his hunger for the outdoors soar through him like a cool mountain breeze. In a matter of moments his mind had taken him back to the streets where he belonged. Home. Walking free.

Later, when the jailer came to let the inmates out for dinner, no one could find Emil. In fact no one even remembered him even being there. He'd vanished into thin air.

Back on the Greenway, Emil brushed himself off trying to get rid of the stink of the jail and said to himself, *I've got to be more careful. I don't know how many more times I can do that.* Then he went back to walking and looking at the sky and the clouds, happy to be outdoors once again. But this time he kept a sharper lookout for cops, because being inside? Well, it just wasn't for him.

Far up ahead, he saw a figure approaching on a bicycle. He looked closely, thinking that might be that cop. "Probably out looking for me," Emil mumbled to himself. He watched as the rider stopped to question a young couple vaping and walking hand in hand. *Yeah, it was him*, he decided, and that was all the motivation Emil needed. He stepped off to the side of the path and disappeared. The cop rode by looking but didn't see anything. He kept on riding. Emil smiled.

Desert Wind

Dave was grateful for the final emotional push as he clamoured up and over the edge of Lizard Peak onto the top, a large flat area.

"Thanks, man," he said to Lyle, his life companion for the last forty years. He was nearly out of breath. "I needed that."

Lyle was also his best friend, and Dave fought back an urge to give him a nostalgic hug. They'd been making this climb for all of those forty years, and right now it felt good to be with him.

Dave walked over to the edge, took off his day pack and turned to admire the view. He never tired of it: the half mile wide spot in the Colorado River known as Lake Havasu; its namesake, Lake Havasu City, a few miles away to his right stretching up into the Sonora desert foothills; the serpentine flow of the Colorado River and, beyond it, the mountains of California rising west into the distance as far as the eye could see. It was a view he never tired of. Birds and hawks and eagles, even the occasional condor, were often seen soaring close enough to touch. Lyle had loved it up here just as much as he did. It was their special place. In fact, it was the first place they'd ever kissed and declared their love for each other. Forty years ago. A lifetime of love, was how Dave looked at it. Their lifetime together now over.

He opened his pack and took out the container that held Lyle's ashes. He'd died less than a week earlier after a mercifully short battle with brain cancer. Dave had been by his side throughout and was there when Lyle had briefly regained consciousness, squeezed Dave's hand and said, "I'll always love you, man." Then, after a few moments, added, "Take me to the desert."

He knew exactly what Lyle had meant.

Dave held the container reverently. There was so much to say that he didn't know where to begin. Finally he spoke to the wind, saying all that was needed: "Lyle, I'll love you forever, my friend. I'll never forget you."

He moved to the edge, six hundred feet above the desert floor, opened the lid and waited. When the wind was right he tilted the container and the ashes spilled out, caught by a sudden gust as if it had been waiting for just that moment. Dave watched as Lyle's ashes swirled away out over the desert that had formed the backdrop for their lifelong love. Then he put the container away and made ready to climb back down. He knew he'd be back. He was already planning for his next trip. He would scale the mountain and stand in the wind. He would overlook the land and be with Lyle, and tell him once again how much he missed him and how much now and forever he would always love him.

Flowers

"Your daughter loves them," Laura said, setting our one-year-old down in the grass next to the patio. Arial immediately grabbed a dandelion and jammed it in her mouth, happily gumming it to death. Laughing, my wife gently pulled the slimy thing out, saying "She also likes petunias", as our little girl grabbed for one from a nearby planter. I reached for her and missed as she swallowed it whole.

Then suddenly she was everywhere, crawling here and there, stuffing flowers in her mouth non-stop, a whirling dervish of floral mastication. It was impossible to try to control her. Frustrated, I was about ready to put a halt to the whole thing and take her inside, when she stopped and looked at me, her blue eyes twinkling in the sunlight. She smiled a flowery smile as she reached out her little hand and offered me a recently plucked yellow daisy. Then she called me, "Daddy." My heart melted as I took it from her while, giggling, she put one in her mouth and started chewing. I didn't have to think. I popped mine in and ate it. It tasted like a burst of pure joy.

Soup Duty

Granny set a steaming plate of pancakes in front of me and said, "Tyler, I need your help later this morning. We've got to go to the church."

No way, I thought, my mouth watering as I drowned the pancakes in maple syrup. "What about painting the house?" I dug in and started eating while looking at my grandfather. I was twelve years old and painting my grandparents' house was going to be my job for the foreseeable future.

He pointed a finger at me and said, "That can wait. For now you do what your grandma says."

I looked at Granny. She was a solidly-built woman with an energetic manner and a cheerful disposition who ran the house in a brisk, no-nonsense manner. Even my grandfather gave into her will and he was the chief of police in the little town where I'd be spending the summer.

I finished breakfast without another word and certainly not a complaint. Granny was her own force to be reckoned with and her mind was made up. We went.

I suppose what I expected was a few old ladies drinking coffee while idly dumping the occasional can of soup into a saucepan and giving it a half-hearted stir. Well, I was wrong. Big time.

Fairmont was the county seat for the farming communities in Martin County, but small enough so we could walk to the church. Granny and I went in through the backdoor and down the stairs into the refreshingly cool basement where my senses were immediately assaulted by the mouth-watering scent of cooking: chicken frying, bread baking and an underlying aroma of something delicious, which turned out to be the soup I was going to help prepare.

"This is Tyler my grandson," Granny said, introducing me to a stern-looking woman built like a fireplug and dressed in a red flowered muumuu.

"Tyler." She nodded at me perfunctorily while thrusting a twelve-inch knife in my direction. I actually jumped back a step, which made her laugh. "Don't have to worry, my boy. We're all friends here." She looked at Granny and said, "I'll get him started." She led me over to a cutting table. "Here you go, young man. You and Deloris are on carrot duty."

"Hi." Deloris nodded in greeting, chopping away a mile a minute and not missing a beat. She was a rail thin woman dressed in bib overalls and a white T-shirt. A faded blue bandana kept her long grey streaked hair out of her eyes and she had a cigarette tucked behind her ear. She smelled like sandalwood oil.

She stopped chopping long enough to hand me a carrot from a pile on the table and said, "Here, let me get you started."

She showed me how to hold the carrot with my fingers bent to lessen the chance of cutting them. Then I went to work.

The kitchen was a bee-hive of activity with the twenty or so ladies in constant motion, making the total seem much higher. Soup was being made, bread baked, chicken roasted and salads prepared. Even though I didn't mind chopping carrots, a couple of ladies were in charge of making cookies and I watched them enviously. There was constant talk and laughter and the occasional song was spontaneously sung. "If I Had A Hammer" was the most popular.

Just after noon, a stack of trays appeared and we started dishing up the meal. Each tray received a bowl of soup, a plate with chicken and mashed potatoes, a salad, a piece of bread and a cookie. We carried the trays through swinging doors to a huge room filled with tables where people waited patiently and quietly, mostly women and their children, along with a few older men. I'd never seen anything like it.

I spent the next hour taking food out to the dining area and removing the trays when the plates were clean, which didn't take long. Most everyone thanked me. One young family had a five or six-year-old boy who took a shine to me and showed me his red yoyo.

"Here, Mister," he said, handing it to me.

I smiled at him. He seemed like a good kid and I sat down. "Hi. What's your name?"

He looked at his mother. She nodded and said, "Go ahead. Tell the nice young man."

My ears burned at the compliment. "My name's Eddie," he said.

I shook his hand. "Hi, Eddie. I'm Tyler. Good to meet you."

"Can you work a yoyo?" he asked.

"I can. Do you want me to show you how?"

"That'd be great," he said, frowning. "I'm having some trouble."

I showed him how to make the yoyo stall at the end of the string and how to walk the dog. "Here, you try." I gave it back to him and after about ten minutes he got the hang of it. It was pretty fun.

Later on, we were cleaning up the kitchen when Granny found me and said, "We do this every Thursday."

"Really?" I couldn't believe it. "That's a lot of work," I said.

"It's not so bad," she said, helping me stack some trays off to the side. "It's good for the community."

After what I'd seen that day, I could agree that she had a point.

That night Grandpa asked how it went. A week ago I was back home in the city working on becoming a juvenile delinquent, before being sent by my mom to spend the summer with my grandparents. Now I had just done something I'd never done before; I'd made soup and served it to some needy people and made them happy.

"It went great," I told him.

Granny asked, "You want to go back next week?"

I smiled and said, "I wouldn't miss it for the world."

And we did, every week until I went home in August. It was the best summer I ever had.

Amaryllis

They grow tall in a pot on a sunny window sill. Four soft pink flowers tinged with swirls of red set against a winter background of white. He touches the petals wistfully, thinking of spring and working in the garden. Mood uplifted, he puts on his warm clothes, heads outside and tramps through knee-high drifts to the shed. He pulls it open against an icy wind and gazes longingly at his gardening tools. Just then he notices more snow beginning to fall and sadly reaches for his shovel. Spring's just around the corner, he tells himself. But not today.

Swing Dancing

Swing dancing night at the Long Lake Retirement Home. "It don't mean a thing if it ain't got that swing," sang the singer. Jerry could dig it as he sat off to the side in the community room, watching. One of the orderlies had a boom box set up on a card table and was playing dance music from the thirties and forties. It was the best. In his memory Jerry could picture a long ago nightclub filled with sweaty bodies dancing up a storm, cigarette smoke swirling and the band wailing to the big beat of the drums and the thumping rhythm of the stand-up bass. He tried to contain himself but he couldn't.

When the next song started he turned to his wife. "Let's go cut the rug, Alice," he said, standing up and reaching for her. "Let's get on that dance floor and show them how it's done."

He grinned as she took his hand and stood with him, smiling. How wonderful she looked tonight in her blue and white checked poodle dress, looking like she was born for this, jitterbugging and jiving with him. Swing dancing. What a lucky man he was. He smiled, thinking this must be what heaven was like.

With Alice by his side, Jerry hurried out to the floor ready to dance like there was no tomorrow, ignoring the fact that it'd been fifteen years since Alice had been with him. Fifteen years since she'd passed away from a valiant battle with cancer. But tonight that was all forgotten.

The crowd watched awestruck as Jerry pivoted onto the floor and began jiving to "In the Mood" by Glenn Miller, dancing like crazy, a smile as wide as the keyboard of a piano, as energetic as the wailing of a saxophone. They watched him, all fluid motion and energy, lost in his memory of those long-ago days, swing dancing across the floor with Alice, the love of his life, together again the way it should be, never wanting the music to end.

The Leviathan

In the deepest part of the ocean, the Mariana Trench, there lives a huge beast scientists call the Leviathan. Two men in a research bathyscaphe led a scientific exploration of the trench in the early sixties. The only known photo of the beast was taken at that time, just before radio contact was lost. The image is of the oesophagus of the creature, as the vessel was swallowed whole. The screams of the two scientists to this day still haunt those who heard it. The tragedy has been kept secret. Can you image what would happen if word got out?

At the Clinic

The nervous-looking man stood up, sat down, then went outside, sucked down a smoke, came back in and began pacing. From his chair on the other side of the clinic Larry watched, all the while wondering, *what the hell's the matter with that guy?*

When the vet's assistant came out from the back, Larry stood to greet her. "Here you go, Mr. Sanderson," she said, handing over Cicely. "Your kitty's doing just fine. It was only a little hairball."

"That's a relief." Larry smiled gratefully, nestling his little four-month-old calico to his chest as she began purring loudly. He gestured towards the guy, now sitting, jiggling his legs and twisting a magazine to death. "What's up with him? Is he okay?"

"Oh, yeah, he's fine. Just a little upset. It's half price procedure day today at the clinic. His dog Pete is getting neutered."

Ouch! Larry thought to himself, and felt a sudden, sharp, sympathy pain, remembering a few years ago when he fulfilled his promise to Nancy a week after their second child was born and had the old tubes tied. Not the most pleasant experience he'd ever had.

At the time his wife had not been one bit sympathetic to his plight. He clearly remembered Nancy looking askance at him saying "Suck it up, Larry" as she helped him hobble to their car. "Try giving birth sometime. Twice."

Which was certainly a true statement, and at the time he'd made a wise marital decision not to pursue the matter any further. In fact, he'd put it all out of his mind. Until now.

He cradled Cicely, petting her while casting a consoling eye toward the dog's owner who was holding the now destroyed magazine limply in his hand, staring into space, hands twitching, dealing with his own inner demons. Somewhere deep in the bowels of the clinic a dog barked and the poor guy grimaced and jumped in his chair. Then he grabbed a new magazine to mangle.

Before the memory of his own procedure became too vivid for comfort Larry figured he'd better leave. He paid for Cicely, then thanked the assistant.

"Okay, goodbye," he said.

She patted Cicely on the head and said, "Right. See you next month. Okay?"

Larry stopped short. "Next month?"

"Yes. She's due back then. It's easier when the kitty is younger."

Larry blanched. That's right. Her procedure. He'd conveniently forgotten. "Oh. Sure," he said, voice cracking, perspiration breaking out on his brow. "Right. I'll see you then."

"Be sure to come, okay?" she said, watching a bead of sweat trickle down Larry's forehead. "Call for an appointment," she added.

"Yeah, I will," he managed to stammer. Then he turned, petting Cicely nervously before wiping his brow. He couldn't get out of there fast enough.

As he made his way to the car, Nancy's words come back to him: "Suck it up Larry." He was trying his best, he really was, but he just couldn't shake the vivid memory of "Being under the knife" as he always referred to his operation.

He situated Cicely in her car carrier in the passenger seat and got in behind the wheel, happy to finally be leaving the clinic behind. Then he remembered that it was only a month before he'd have to return. Not good. His hands started shaking at the thought.

Next to him, Cicely started her motor going, purring up a gentle storm, usually a calming influence. But not today. Man, Larry thought to himself, it was becoming obvious he was not very good at this kind of thing, handling these procedures and operations and what not. Maybe he should ask Nancy if she would take Cicely to the clinic for him next month. Then he stopped himself. No. Bad idea. He knew exactly what she'd say. "Don't be such a baby, Larry. Suck it up for God's sake."

Larry sighed and scratched Cicely under her chin through the mesh on the carrier's door. "Don't worry, girl. It'll be just fine. Trust me." In answer, she looked up at him with big blue eyes, her motor going full tilt, purring up a storm. *Bring it on,* she seemed to be saying to him, blinking calmly and casually licking a paw. *Just bring it on.* She kept looking at him, like she was ready for anything; ready to go anytime, whether he was or not.

He patted her head before putting the car in gear. "Good girl," he told Cicely as they left the parking lot. It was up to him to take her back for her procedure. Both Cicely and Nancy were depending on him. He had a month. Plenty of time to get his act together. Plenty of time to figure out how to suck it up. He hoped. Either that or they'd better have some magazines on hand for him to mangle. Make that a lot of magazines.

Dolphins

They were on the back of their cabin cruiser, her husband drinking whiskey and berating her as usual. Suddenly a pod of dolphins surfaced and began following. She marvelled at their graceful beauty while they swam closer, as if listening. Then, in an instant they leapt as one and knocked him into the sea before swimming away.

She watched the jerk sink. "Good riddance," she said, smiling. To the departing dolphins she waved. "Thank you!"

Later, she told the investigating officers, "He slipped and fell overboard. He'd been drinking."

Because if she told them the truth, who'd have believed her?

Freedom

"Hey, Norman, stop!"

"Yeah, you idiot. Don't make this any harder on yourself than it has to be. We don't want to have to hurt you."

Norman glanced over his shoulder. The orderlies he thought of as Huey and Dewey were in hot pursuit but he hitched up his pyjamas and kept running. He was on the West River Road in Minneapolis high above the Mississippi. To his right he caught a glimpse of the river sparkling a hundred feet below in the early morning sunlight. It was a beautiful view, much better that being stuck in the group home two blocks away.

A third voice broke into his thoughts. Louie. The meanest of the orderlies. "I'm going to get you, you crazy fool. Then you'll be sorry."

Damn! He was terrified of being caught and sent back for more injections and medication and counselling. He clutched the urn carrying the remains of his beloved family to his chest and made a snap decision.

"You'll never get me!" he yelled.

Then he leaped over the guard rail and began plummeting down the side of the steep embankment. Behind him he heard the orderlies cursing. *Serves them right*, he smiled. Then he concentrated on not smashing into a tree and killing himself as he rolled over and over and over.

Oddly enough, time seemed to stand still as he rolled. He could see the world so very clearly; the red buds on the sumac bushes, the dried-out bark on the ancient oak trees and the hollowed-out burrow of an animal, possibly a fox. All those images were crystal clear until they sped up and collapsed in upon themselves, turning into a blur, like an old-time motion picture that had jumped the reel.

A branch slapped him in the face and he ducked. Then another one, this one catching him across the cheekbone momentarily stunning him and opening a wound. He wiped blood from his eyes to try and clear his vision.

He kept tumbling, crashing through bushes and getting smacked by branches, all the while unwilling to let go of the urn clutched to his chest, the ashes of his wife and son and daughter; his darling Ann and young Ethan and Leslie, killed by a drunk driver on the way back from soccer practice, while he'd stayed home and cooked them a surprise spaghetti dinner. Upon hearing the news he'd collapsed and hadn't been the same since. The doctors told him he'd had a complete breakdown. Post-traumatic stress disorder they'd called it. He couldn't handle the loss and the pain and the despair of having lost the three people he'd loved most in the world. That had been over two years ago.

But no more. Now he was free. Now he could be with Ann and Ethan and Leslie on his own terms and not under the watchful eyes of the doctors and nurses and those three crazy orderlies.

Above the river was a ten-foot drop over the edge of a limestone outcropping. Norman tumbled off it and crashed onto a sandy shoreline holding his urn tightly. The landing knocked the wind out of him. Dazed, he lay on his back, semi-conscious, looking up at the sky and watching gulls float overhead against a brilliant blue sky. He caressed his urn and smiled. He was almost free.

He got to his feet and brushed leaves and other debris from his pyjamas, then stepped to the edge of the river and bent down, splashing water on his face, washing the blood off. Behind him, coming fast down the embankment he heard the cursing and yelling from Huey, Dewey and Louie. They would be on him in seconds. Panicking, he did the only thing he could think of; he stepped into the river.

He was about to start swimming when he noticed a partially submerged log floating downstream toward him. He gave a silent cheer as he stepped in further up to his waist. The water felt good, cool and refreshing and natural, not like the smelly chloride loaded stuff at the group home.

He gripped his urn tightly and was just reaching for the log when a strong hand grabbed him by the shoulder. "All right there, Norman. I've got you. You aren't going anywhere. Let's get you back to the home."

At the sound of Louie's voice, Norman shook himself awake and opened his eyes. What he saw shocked him because he wasn't in the river preparing to swim to freedom anymore. Instead, he was lying flat on his back on his bed in his room at the group home with Louie holding his shoulders down, looming over him like a deranged beast.

Norman raised his head and looked around. On either side of him were Huey and Dewey. *What was going on? Had he been dreaming?* He looked frantically for his urn and spied it on the dresser like always. He breathed a sigh of relief. *Good. His family was still with him.*

"He's finally coming around," Louie was saying. "He's in bad shape. The doctor might want to adjust this weirdo's meds."

"The nurse is on the way," Huey said.

"Yeah with something to calm him down," Dewey added.

Their pointless chatter filled the room and Norman closed his eyes, tuning them out. In his mind he hadn't been dreaming; it had been too real. He was sick to death of being treated like a nutcase. Right then and there he vowed he was going back to the river. He needed to escape and knew that he could. He just had to be quicker. A plan formed as the nurse entered the room to give him a sedative. He kept his eyes shut while Louie held him down and the nurse slipped the needle in his vein. Next time he'd grab his urn and run faster. They'll never catch him. Next time he'd get away for good.

No More Killing

The man sighted down the rifle barrel. The animal froze. Their eyes locked and he noticed a twinkle in its eye as the little cottontail softly blinked.

He lowered the gun. "Dad, what are you doing?" his son asked.

"I've had it. No more killing."

"What are you going to do?"

He walked to the garage, put the rifle in a vice and grabbed a hacksaw. "What's it look like?" He pulled blade across the barrel and began sawing.

"Good," his son grinned with relief. "I liked that bunny." Then he grabbed his own saw and started in. "I'll help."

'Twas the Night Before Christmas

With five-year-old Stacy and three-year-old Dale nestled snug under the covers beside him, Cole was the happiest he'd been in months. He opened his treasured book, one passed down from his grandmother to his mom and then to him. He cleared his throat and began to read, his voice quiet as a whisper, drawing his young ones in, "'Twas the night before Christmas and all through the house, not a creature was stirring, not even a mouse…"

By the time he'd finished, both children were asleep, breathing restfully with visions, Cole hoped, of sugar plums dancing in their heads. He smiled to himself. *Why not? It was Christmas Eve, as good a time for magical thoughts as any.*

He tucked them under their warm covers and, before turning out the light, paused at the doorway, taking a long moment watching his two little sleepy heads. Worn out from seeing Dad, he joked to himself, hoping it was true. It was. Just ask Lyn, his wife. She'd say that their children adored their father and missed him terribly while he was away getting his treatments. Then she'd get a little teary eyed, her strength wavering ever so slightly before returning, knowing there were still more long days to come.

After turning out the bedroom light, Cole made his way to the stairway and began to descend, step by cautious step, holding onto the handrail with what little strength he had. From the living room, Lyn saw him and hurried to help. "Here, Sweetheart, lean on me. We'll go slow. We can rest together on the couch."

He smiled, grateful for everything about her. "That'd be perfect."

It took a few minutes before they were finally curled up together under the wool Afghan Lyn had knitted when they were first married, seven years earlier. The room was a peaceful sanctuary, with Christmas music playing so quietly in the background they had to strain to hear a choir singing, "Silent night, holy night, all is calm, all is bright." Lyn had turned off all the lights except for the warm glow from the Christmas tree. It was lit with white twinkling lights, and decorated with a myriad of coloured glass ornaments and handmade decorations, accented with at least five strands of popcorn and cranberries. The family had decorated it that afternoon when Cole had come home from the hospital on a twenty-four-hour pass.

Lyn put her head on his shoulder. "Isn't the tree beautiful?"

"It's our best tree ever," he smiled, putting a thin arm around her and holding her tight.

He liked that Lyn was willing to put aside what was really happening with his disease, at least for tonight. Tonight, he had a break from his treatments. Tonight, he could be home with his family and enjoy a moment of comfort and repose before leaving tomorrow to go back to the hospital to continue his battle. There was so much he wanted to tell her, but he was getting tired so he said only what he needed to say, "Lyn, I love you so much. You mean the world to me."

It was all Lyn needed to hear. She kissed him gently. "I love you, too, Cole. Forever and always."

He kissed her in return. Their undying affection for each other carrying them through these most challenging of times.

They must have fallen asleep. A rustle on the stairway caused Cole to awaken. He turned to see his children, standing patiently, so young and so innocent, dressed in their red flannel pyjamas. Stacy was holding a book, and Cole could see it was the one he'd read to them earlier.

"Daddy, could you read to us again?" she asked, her tiny voice music to his ears.

"Please, Daddy, please," Dale chimed in.

Their voices woke Lyn. "The kids want me to read again," Cole said to her, sitting up and stretching. "I know it's late, but is it all right with you?"

Lyn didn't have to think. "Absolutely. But first," she said, getting to her feet, "how about if I fix us a plate of ginger cookies and some milk for a little treat? How would everyone like that?"

Three heads nodded enthusiastically, and all was well for them on this Christmas Eve, the world held at bay for a little while longer.

Later, the family snuggled together on the couch under the warm Afghan, leftover cookies within easy reach. Cole began the story, wondering as he read if this would be the last time he'd be able to do this, reading to his family as was now. Then he put the thought out of his mind. *Quit thinking like that*, he admonished himself. He had to stay positive. He had to believe that he'd be with his wife and children next year. After all, who else could read "'Twas the Night Before Christmas" to his children like he could? No one.

"Merry Christmas to all and to all a good night," he said, when he reached the end of the story, but not before adlibbing a hearty "Ho, ho, ho", making the kids giggle and Lyn smile.

Then he closed the book and wrapped his arms around his wife and children and hugged his family all together as tightly as he could. "Until next year," he whispered to himself. "Until next year."

The Kingfisher

Years ago, I watched a boy as he took his first tentative steps before learning to walk. Then run. I saw his eyes fill with wonder, as the world opened up before him. All those possibilities – a lifetime ahead.

Today, I watched an old lady take her last tentative steps. Slowly shuffling, breathing laboured and heart weakening, she took my hand and we walked together. I imagined her thinking her thoughts, now turned inward, of the times she ran, and danced, and rode her bicycle, and hiked in the mountains. Her world has shrunk now, but she doesn't complain.

After a while, she and I sat and rested and talked, and I saw those memories come alive: the twinkle in her eye ignited and flaming, the breathing less laboured, and the memories of the past sparkling clearly in her renewed vision. She was calm and at peace. Time slowed to a crawl. I moved to hold her hand, happy to be with her.

Later, she and I watched a Kingfisher. It was perched on a branch overlooking a slough just starting to break free from winter's frozen grip. He was among the first wave of spring migrants, in his own way showing a complete faith and total belief that food will be found, and eventually a mate, and his cycle of life will continue. He looked confident as he suddenly dived into the icy water, hunting, and, for that moment, I felt the joy of being reminded that somehow, no matter what, life will continue to go on.

She turned to me and smiled. "Can we stay awhile?"

"Sure," I said, smiling right back at her. "For as long as you want."

"Good," she said.

Like to Read More Work Like This?

Then sign up to our mailing list and download our free collection of short stories, *Magnetism*. Sign up now to receive this free e-book and also to find out about all of our new publications and offers.

Sign up here:
   http://eepurl.com/gbpdVz

Please Leave a Review

Reviews are so important to writers. Please take the time to review this book. A couple of lines is fine.

Reviews help the book to become more visible to buyers. Retailers will promote books with multiple reviews.

This in turn helps us to sell more books… And then we can afford to publish more books like this one.

Leaving a review is very easy. Go to https://smarturl.it/6sgrt6, scroll down the left-hand side of the Amazon page and click on the "Write a customer review" button.

Other Books by Jim Bates

Resilience

Remembrance Day is special for one grandfather. Which story of he and his brother at the lake will John remember today? Blake loves his garden but he's not so sure about the rabbit. Tyler stands up to his dad while hunting crows. What really did happen in the room at the Inn on the Lake? Why doesn't Quinn run away anymore?

"*Resilience* is an absolute gem. A collection of twenty-seven beautifully written short stories that deal with the central theme of its title." *(Amazon)*

Order from Amazon:

ISBN: 978-1-914199-00-4 (paperback)
978-1-914199-01-1 (ebook)

Periodic Stories
Published by Impspired

The first thirty-one elements of the periodic table are each used in the thirty-one stories in this unique collection. Will Warren always be lonely? How come Derek's new fishing rod is so important to him? How did Eric's spoon melt when he stirred the coffee? These are lovingly written stories that deal with human beings and their relationship with themselves and others. Oh, yes, sometimes science plays a role.

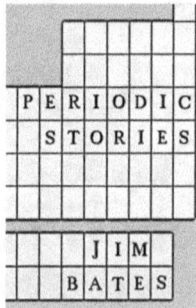

"I loved this book – it's my total favourite, and I read a lot." *(Amazon)*

Order from Amazon:

ISBN: 978-1-914130-08-3 (paperback)
ASIN: B08Z8CYNLB (ebook)

Read More of Jim's Work in These Books

The Best of CaféLit 8
Published by Chapeltown Books

Order from Amazon:

Paperback: ISBN 978-1-907335-76-1
eBook: ISBN 978-1-910542-46-0

The Best of CaféLit 9
Published by Chapeltown Books

Order from Amazon:

Paperback: ISBN 978-1-910542-54-5
eBook: ISBN 978-1-910542-55-2

Mulling It Over
Published by Bridge House

Order from Amazon:

Paperback: ISBN 978-1-907335-93-8
eBook: ISBN 978-1-907335-94-5

Nativity
Published by Bridge House

    Order from Amazon:

    Paperback: ISBN 978-1-907335-76-1
    eBook: ISBN 978-1-907335-77-8

Covid 19: An Extraordinary Time
Published by Chapeltown Books

    Order from Amazon:

    Hardback: ISBN 978-1-910542-72-9
    eBook: ISBN 978-1-910542-73-6

For more buying options see the Bridgetown Café Bookshop at
<u>www.thebridgetowncafebooksshop.co.uk/search/label/Jim%20Bates</u>